D0990034

John Ciardi

THE WISH-TREE

Illustrated by Louis S. Glanzman

A MODERN MASTERS BOOK FOR CHILDREN
THE CROWELL-COLLIER PRESS

First Crowell-Collier Press Edition 1962

Library of Congress Catalog Card Number: 62-21619
Copyright ©1962 by The Crowell-Collier Publishing Company

All Rights Reserved
Hecho en los E.E.U.U.
Printed in the United States of America

I was going to bed and I was happy.

No, I am not always happy when I have to go to bed. But this night I was as happy as I could be.

It was my last night to be five years old. When I woke up, I would be six!

That is why I was happy. There are not many times,
after all, when you can go to bed five and wake up six!
I was going to have a birthday!

There would be a birthday cake. There would be
toys.

There would be a lot of good things. And maybe…
just maybe…

there would be a little brown puppy. I had wished and wished for a little brown puppy. Oh, how I had wished and wished for one!

"What a lot of wishes you are wishing," Daddy said as I got into bed. "I see you will just have to find a Wish–Tree." Then he told me all about Wish–Trees. He told me all about the Wish–Trees he had found when he was small. Then he sat on my bed and began to tuck me in.

"Daddy," I said, "could I find a Wish–Tree?"

Daddy stopped tucking me in and looked at me. "Anyone can find a Wish–Tree," he said. "All you have to do is look for one. Why don't you look and see if you can find one?"

"Oh, I will!" I said. "I will!"

"There is just one thing," Daddy said. "When you find a Wish-Tree you must look at it well. If it is a true Wish-Tree you will find something cut into the trunk of the tree. I must not tell you what it is. You must find that out as best you can. Not until you find out can you make a true wish."

"But how will I know what it is?" I said.

Daddy picked up my pad and wrote on it. "This is what you will find cut into the trunk of the tree," he said. And he gave me the pad. On it I saw:

TAKECAREOFYOURWISH

What a big word!

"What is *that?*" I said.

"That," said Daddy, "is what you have to find out. For not until you do find out can you make a true wish."

"But it looks too big for me to find out about!" I said.

Daddy tucked me in and kissed me. "You think about it," he said. "You will find out what it means. I know you will, if you just think about it."

And then he put out the light and went away.

Well, I did think about it.

I lay in my bed, thinking and thinking. It was dark, but I could still see what Daddy had put on my pad. I could see it in my head.

But how could I find out about anything that big? And how could I make a true wish if I did not find out? And how could I find my true Wish–Tree? I lay in my bed, thinking and thinking and thinking.

But what good does it do to think about something too big for you? I tried and tried to think what it might be. I lay in my bed, and I could see it. I could see it in my head. But I still could not tell what it was.

"Oh, well," I said, "it is too much for me. I will just think about Wish–Trees."

And I wished and I wished and I wished that I might find out.

Oh, how I did wish for one!
I wished and I wished till I could all but see one.

I wished and I wished till my wish grew into a cloud.

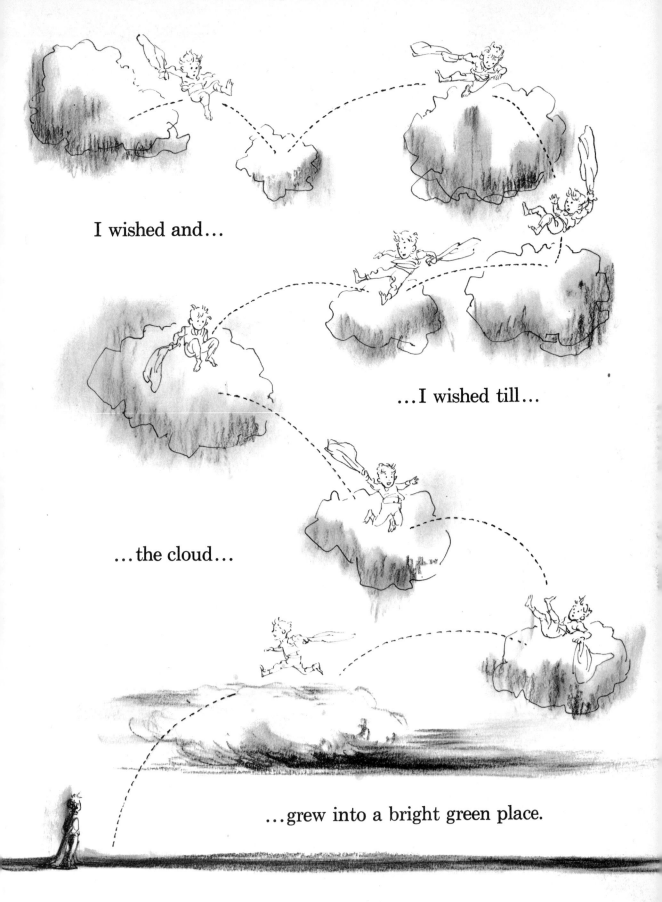

I wished and...

...I wished till...

...the cloud...

...grew into a bright green place.

I wished and I wished till I found I could go right into that bright green place.

And when I had gone into it...
there was my WISH–TREE!

Oh, what a tree it was!

It was as big around as a hill!

It was so tall the sky had to bump up

to get over the top of it.

The trunk of my Wish–
Tree was as big as a house.
    I went up to that trunk as
big as a house, and there was
a little door cut into it.

I went up to that little door…

and it got bigger…

and bigger.

I went up to the door and looked at it.
I looked way up to the top of the door
and I saw something cut into the trunk.
It was cut into the trunk around the top
of the door. It looked like this:

That is how I knew it was a true Wish–Tree! For
what was cut into the trunk above the door was just
what Daddy had put down on my pad!

But what did it mean? I tried and I tried to think
what it might mean.

But what good does it do to think about something
too big for you? I knew I had found a true Wish–Tree,
and I had a lot of wishing to get done, and the door
was open!

In I went.

As soon as I went in I saw
some steps. A lot of steps.
There were more steps than I
could see, and more steps than
I could count, and more steps
than I could think about.

How many steps do you think it would take to get to the top of a wish?

That is how many steps there were.

I went up one flight of steps and found
a place as big as my room. And there I
saw a little brown puppy sitting still.

"Hello," said the little brown puppy, "I knew you would come."

"But how could you know that?" I said.

"You wished me a long time ago," said the little brown puppy, "and I belong to you. What sort of puppy could I be if no one wished for me?"

" I don't think I know about that," I said, "but it is true that I did wish for you. Oh, how I did wish and wish for you."

"There," said the little brown puppy, "do you see?"
And he licked my hand and gave a high-little, glad-
little, funny-little puppy-bark.

And then he sang me this song:

You have to wish and wish for me
And I will wish and wish for you.
What sort of puppy could I be
If no one wished and wished for me?
But the wish you wish will not come true
Till you know the word on the Wish–Tree
But when you do, oh, when you do,
I will be wishing there for you.

"Do you mean," I said, "that you have been my puppy from the time I first wished for you, and that I did not find you until now?"

"Go up one more flight," said the little brown puppy, "and see what you will find there. Bit by bit you will find out all you wish to know."

"Won't you come with me?" I said. "Please do."

"Not now," said the little brown puppy licking my hand. "I have to stay here in this part of your wish till you find out what all your wish is."

"May I say I don't know what all that means?" I
said.

"Bit by bit," said the little brown puppy. And he
gave my hand a last lick and sat down again just as
he had been sitting when I came in.

I went up another flight and came to a green place
as big as my yard.

It was all full of growing things and it was as bright
as roses. There were birds in all the green places.

There were red birds,

blue birds,

black birds,

cat birds,

jay birds,

yellow birds,

white birds,

and more birds.

There were birds everywhere I looked, and more birds than I could count.

How many birds does it take to fill all of a wish?
That is how many birds there were.

And all of them were singing a sad, sad song in the trees. "Why do such bright birds sing such a sad song?" I said.

I said it out loud without knowing I had said it.

As if they had heard me, the biggest white bird and the biggest black bird flew down from their green places in the trees. The biggest white bird picked a red rose from the red rose bush. The biggest black bird picked a white rose from the white rose bush. Then the biggest white bird and the biggest black bird flew out over the grass and dropped the roses.

And where the roses fell, I saw a brown dog with long ears made of silk.

The brown dog lay on the grass.

"Are you sick?" I said, going up to the brown dog and putting my hand on his head.

The brown dog with the long ears made of silk looked up at me without moving his head.

"I love you all the same," he said, "but you have to take care of your wish. That is why I could not come to you when you were down there. I had to stay in that part of your wish till you could find out what all of your wish is."

"Oh," I said, "what have I done!"

I think I was beginning to understand.

And just then all the birds began to sing:

Roses white and roses red,
Wishes and puppies do come true.
But they have to be tended, they have to be fed.
Or little brown dogs, and wishes too,
Fade and die, and when they are dead,
What can you say, and what can you do
But sing them a song and drop on their head
Roses white and roses red?

And out of all the bright birds there flew a great
black crow who said:

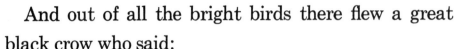

"*You should have
taken care of him!*"

"Oh, please," I said, "I did love him! I have always loved him! I did not know he was sick!"

"*Too late,*" said the big black crow.

"I will do anything to make him well," I said. "May I take him back with me and try? For I will make him well. I will! I will! May I take him with me, please?"

"He has to stay here in this part of your wish," said the big black crow. "Go up one more flight."

"Oh, please," I said. "Won't you let me take him with me?"

"One more flight," said the big black crow. "Do as you are told!" And it flew back into its green place in the trees.

I went up another flight, crying a little, and I came to a place as big as a park. There was grass as far as I could see. And there was a blue lake as bright as glass.

Someone was flying a kite high in the sky, but I could not see who it was. The kite dipped and rose, dipped and rose, higher and higher after each dip.

But as high as it flew, I could still see the steps of my wish going still higher into the sky.

"Ah," I said, without having to think about it, "I know what that means!" For, do you see, there just cannot be any top to a wish. There is always one more place for the steps to go up to. There just have to be more steps, and then more…

…and then more.

"But I don't wish to go any higher," I said out loud, without knowing I was saying it. "Not now."

"I just want the little brown puppy to grow up and be a brown dog with long ears made of silk," I said. "I just want him to be well, and to play with me. And I will take good care of him. I will! I will!"

And just as I said that, I looked to my right and there was Daddy holding the kite string. He pulled the kite down bit by bit, till the kite became a box.

And then down, bit by bit, till the box lay on the grass.

And then he opened the box.

And out of the box jumped the brown dog with long ears made of silk!

He gave a glad bark and came running to me and licked my hand and gave another glad bark.

"See?" he said. "I did get well. You did care, didn't you?"

And he licked my hand again and said, "Go back now. I have to stay in this part of your wish. But I will be here when you come back to me."

"Oh, please stay!" I cried.

"I will. I will," said the brown dog with long ears made of silk. "I will stay here in this part of your wish until you come back to it."

"Right now," he said, "you must go back to the part of your wish that has a little brown puppy in it."

"But please," he said, "do not forget what the birds sang!"

And off he ran giving off his glad bark. Round and
round the bright blue lake he ran while the wind wrote
on the water:

"So *that's* what it means!" I cried.

And the wind sang:

Take care of your wish, and if you do
Your wish will be there just for you.
It will
    it will
       it will
        ...it will...

The song grew smaller and smaller till it sank away
into nothing at all.

And as I was trying to be as still as can be, thinking that maybe I might still hear it, Daddy shook me, and I was back in my bed!

"Happy Birthday, Six-Year-Old!" Daddy said. And he gave me a big hug.

And then I heard a high-little, glad-little, funny-little puppy-bark.

And there on my bed was the little brown puppy!

"My goodness," said Daddy, "there is a little brown puppy on your bed."

"I see you must have found your Wish-Tree!"

"Oh Daddy," I said, "I did! I did! *And I found out what the big word is!*"

"I knew you would," said Daddy.

And the little brown puppy ran up the bed and licked my face and gave a high-little, glad-little, funny-little puppy-bark!